Twinkle, Twinkle, Little Star

by Jane Taylor

Illustrated by Julia Noonan

Cartwheel
B·O·O·K·S ™

SCHOLASTIC INC.

New York   Toronto   London   Auckland   Sydney

ISBN 0-590-45928-7

Illustrations copyright © 1992 by Julia Noonan.
All rights reserved. Published by Scholastic Inc.
CARTWHEEL BOOKS is a trademark of Scholastic Inc.

10 9 8 7 6 5 4 3 2 1   2 3 4 5 6 7/9

Printed in the U.S.A.   09

First Scholastic printing, October 1992

To John, who has always made my
Christmas wishes come true

Special thanks to Jim Roginski

*T*winkle, twinkle, little star,

How I wonder what you are!

★

Up above the world so high,

Like a diamond in the sky.

★

When the blazing sun is gone,

When he nothing shines upon,

★

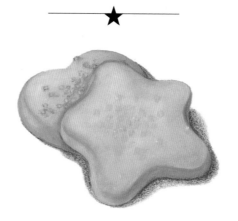

Then you show your little light,

Twinkle, twinkle, all the night.

★

Then the traveller in the dark,

Thanks you for your tiny spark;

★

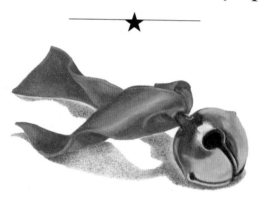

NOONAN © 92

He could not see which way to go,

If you did not twinkle so.

★

In the dark blue sky you keep,

And often through my curtains peep,

★

For you never shut your eye,

Till the sun is in the sky.

★

As your bright and tiny spark,

Lights the traveller in the dark,

★

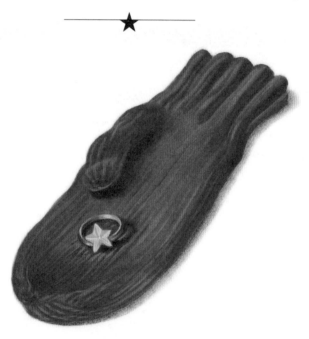

Though I know not what you are,

Twinkle, twinkle, little star.

★

© 92 NOONAN

Twinkle, Twinkle, Little Star